Written by Gaby Goldsack
Illustrated by Steve Smallman

This edition published by Parragon in 2009

Parragon
Queen Street House
4 Queen Street
Bath BA1 1HE, UK

ISBN 978-1-4054-1501-9
Printed in China

Missing Milk

Illustrated by Steve Smallman

Bath · New York · Singapore · Hong Kong · Cologne · Delhi · Melbourne

Farmer Fred was feeling very pleased with himself.

"I'm not one to boast," he told his wife Jenny, "but I'm sure my singing is doing Connie Cow a world of good. She's grown very plump around the middle. And she's giving me buckets of milk."

Jenny looked at Connie. "Hmm. Do you suppose she could be...?"

But Farmer Fred was too busy singing to listen.

The next day, as Connie waddled towards the milking-shed, the other farm animals gossiped amongst themselves.

"I'm sure she's getting fatter," clucked Hetty Hen.

"You don't suppose that she's having a baby, do you?" asked Harry Horse. The animals began to chatter with excitement.

A week later, Farmer Fred wasn't feeling so pleased with himself.

"Connie's run out of milk," he moaned. "Perhaps I'm singing the wrong songs."

Moo!

He closed his eyes and burst into song. Connie mooed loudly. She wished Farmer Fred could be quieter.

"Old MacDonald had a cow,
But not as good as mine!
For Connie's creamy milk is best
And always tastes real fine!"

"I just don't understand it," said Farmer Fred. "Where has her milk gone?"

The animals tried to tell Farmer Fred that Connie had a new calf who was drinking all Connie's milk. But Farmer Fred just looked puzzled at all the noise.

"He just doesn't understand," sighed Harry Horse, stamping his hoof and knocking over the bucket.

Farmer Fred's eyes lit up.

"Yes, that's got to be it! We've got a milk thief on the farm!" cried Farmer Fred. "But never fear, I've an idea!"

Farmer Fred disappeared into his workshop. There were sounds of drawers opening and closing, and cupboard doors banging.

All the animals looked on, wondering what was happening.

"What's Farmer Fred up to now?" asked Polly Pig.

Finally, Farmer Fred came out holding a large ball of string that he had found.

"I'm going to set a trap to catch that milk thief," he said. Farmer Fred got a really long piece of string and tied one end to the gate leading to Cowslip Meadow.

When Farmer Fred went to bed
that night, he tied the other end of
the string to his big toe.

As Farmer Fred settled into bed,
Jenny couldn't help chuckling.

"Fred, are you sure Connie's
not just...?" But Farmer Fred
was already fast asleep.

ZZZzz

He had only been sleeping for a few minutes when he felt a tug at his toe.

"Thundering turnips!" grunted Farmer Fred, hopping out of bed. He peered through the window. But it was only an owl perching on the string.

"Get off my string," shouted Farmer Fred, wiggling the string.

Soon there was so much noise that everyone woke up.

The next morning everyone on the farm was very, very tired. Hetty Hen called a farmyard meeting. Everyone but Connie was there.

"It's time Farmer Fred found out the truth about Connie. Otherwise we'll never get any peace around here," yawned Hetty Hen.

"Patch, it's up to you," neighed Harry Horse. "Farmer Fred always listens to you."

That night, Farmer Fred stood guard with his pitchfork in Cowslip Meadow.

"No one's going to get away with stealing my milk," he muttered.

Very slowly, and very carefully, he began counting the cows.

"One, two, *yawn...*" All this counting was making him sleepy. "Three, four, *yawn...zzzz*" He was fast asleep before he'd even reached five.

But Patch wasn't going to let Farmer Fred snooze the night away.

"Woof, woof!" he barked.

"What? Where?" cried Farmer Fred, suddenly waking up.

"Woof, woof!" Patch set off up the field barking over his shoulder at Farmer Fred.

"Do you want me to follow you, Patch?" asked Farmer Fred sleepily. "Have you found that milk thief?"

Patch led Farmer Fred to the old barn at the top of the field.

Farmer Fred shone his torch around the barn. And there in the corner was Connie. Beside her was the milk thief – a beautiful baby calf.

"Aah! You've got a little calf to feed!"
cried Farmer Fred. "No wonder you had
no milk to spare, Connie!"

The next day, Farmer Fred was feeling very pleased with himself.

"I'm not one to boast," he told Jenny, "but I just knew Connie was going to have a calf. After all, she was looking very plump!"

Jenny and Patch looked at each other and rolled their eyes.

Harry, Hetty, Polly, Shirley and all the other animals smiled happily. Now, perhaps, they could all get some sleep!